H. MAZES

SUZANNE ROSS

DOVER PUBLICATIONS, INC.
Mineola, New York

Bibliographical Note

Halloween Mazes is a new work, first published by
Dover Publications, Inc., in 1998.

International Standard Book Number
ISBN-13: 978-0-486-40208-6
ISBN-10: 0-486-40208-8

Manufactured in the United States by LSC Communications
40208813   2020
www.doverpublications.com

NOTE

Ready for some Halloween fun? Here are lots of mazes with witches, ghosts, pumpkins, merry monsters, kids trick-or-treating, and more. Be sure to read the directions before you try to solve the mazes (it's more fun that way!) and you can color the maze-pictures when you're through. Solutions start on p. 52 (but no peeking, please).

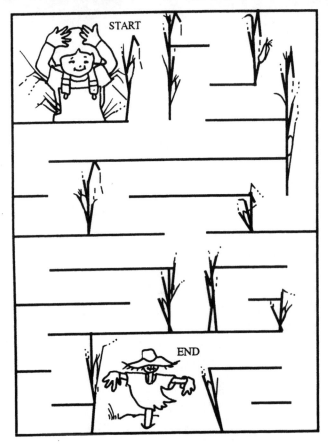

Eliza wants to borrow the scarecrow's hat for her Halloween costume. Help her find it at the other side of the cornfield.

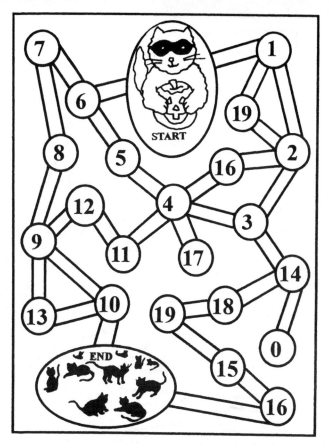

If he follows the correct path of numbers,
1 through 10, Boo the cat will be able
to join the cats' party.

Follow the path to see what costume
Jack decided to wear for Halloween.

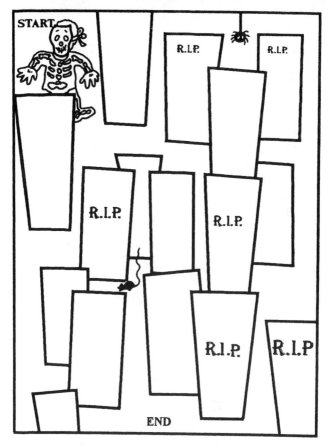

Jennifer is dressed as a skeleton. She can't
find her way through the cemetery.
Can you help?

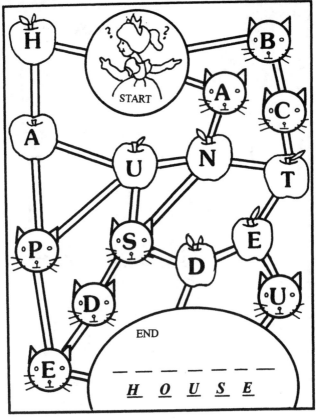

END

_ _ _ _ _
_H_ _O_ _U_ _S_ _E_

Emily needs help reading the secret
Halloween message. Collect all of the letters
along the apple path without touching
the cat path. Then write the letters
in order in the spaces below.

Help the witch collect all of the herbs to finish her magic potion—but don't cross any goblins on the way.

9

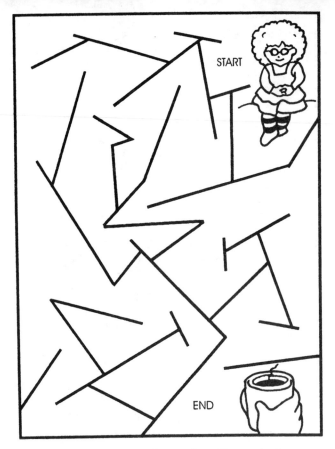

START

END

This Halloweener, dressed as Raggedy Ann,
needs help to reach her cocoa treat.

START

END

Joey wants to be a king for Halloween.
He has a robe but he can't find the rest of
his costume. Show him the path.

11

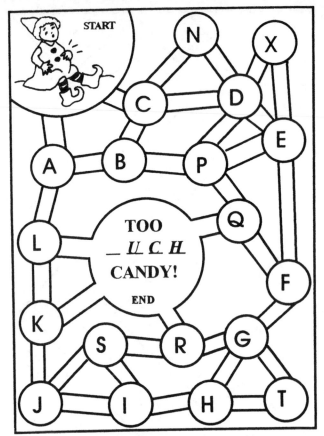

START

TOO
_ U C H
CANDY!

END

A letter is missing to tell us why this goblin is feeling sick. Gather the letters in alphabetical order to the end. Then fill in the blank with the next letter of the alphabet.

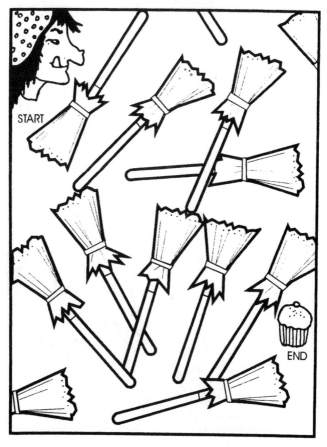

Help this witch find a path through
the brooms so she can eat the
cupcake at the end.

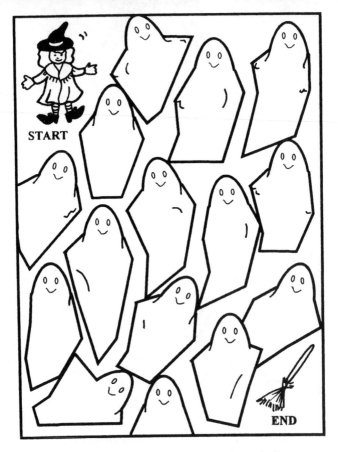

Amanda is dressed as a witch and she
needs her broom. Please help her
get past all of the ghosts.

Show this Halloween cat how
to find his toy mouse.

15

Help this Halloween bunny reach
his squirrel friend.

16

Can you guide one masked
Halloweener to the other?

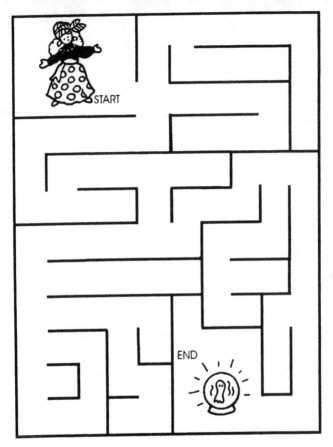

This fortune-teller needs her crystal ball for
Halloween, but she needs your help to find it.

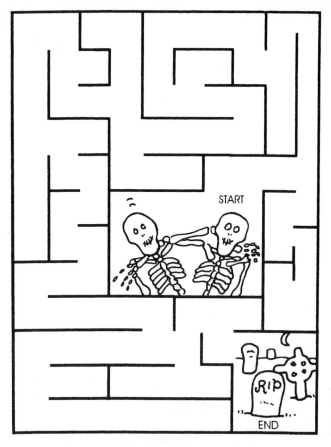

Please guide these paper skeletons
to a Halloween cemetery.

START

END

Frankenstein needs his shoes to complete
his Halloween costume. Can you
help him find them?

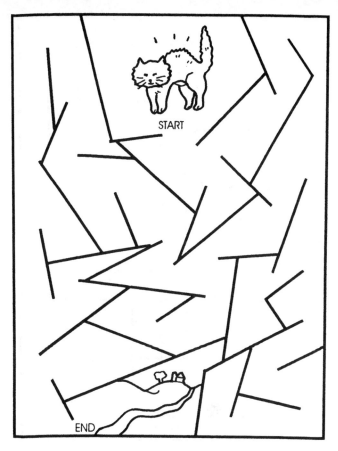

Show this scaredy-cat how to find the country
so he can escape from Halloween.

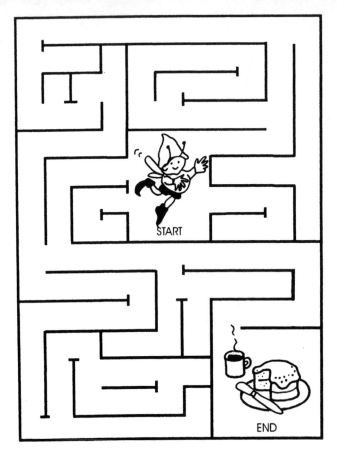

Here's a goblin who needs your help to find
the leftover Halloween cake and cocoa.

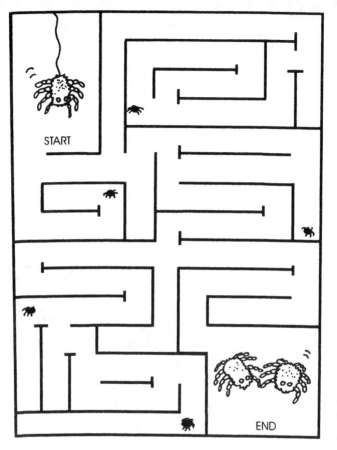

START

END

Guide this lonely spider to his friend's
Halloween party, but don't go near
any spiders along the way.

23

One witch would like to visit the other. Can
you help her find the path to her friend?

The web really bugs these Halloweeners.
Show them how to reach each other.

START

END

Ariel wants to be a fairy princess for
Halloween. Help her find a wand.

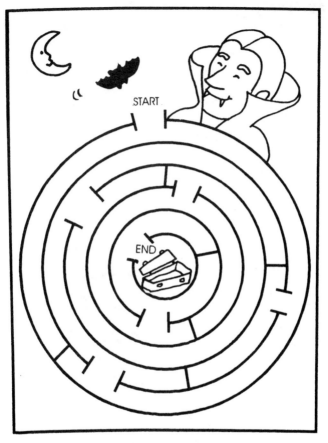

Count Dracula wants to take a nap in
his coffin bed before Halloween.
Can you show him the way?

27

Help a blindfolded Victoria find
her way through the bats.

Guide Heidi along the path to the
end of the candy corn.

START

END

Matt is dressed as an astronaut. He needs
help to find the path so he can finish his
spaceship in time for Halloween.

The cowboy and fortune-teller
are looking for Halloween treats.
Can you help them find some?

31

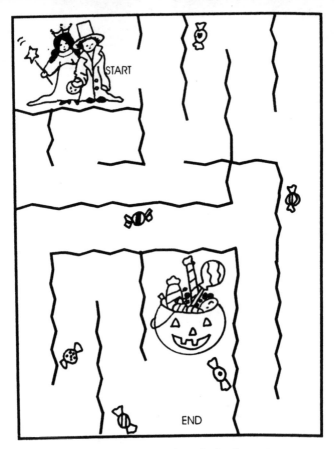

Follow the candy path to help these two
Halloweeners find their first goodies of the day.

This Halloween lion could use a drink of cold cider. You can guide him there by following the drops of cider.

START

END

Help these two children find the path to
something they need for Halloween.

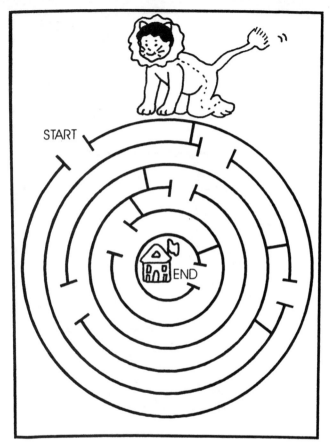

Chris wants to reach the school Halloween
party. Help him follow the path.

START

END

Help this mysterious Halloweener
reach the bowl of popcorn by
following the path of popcorn.

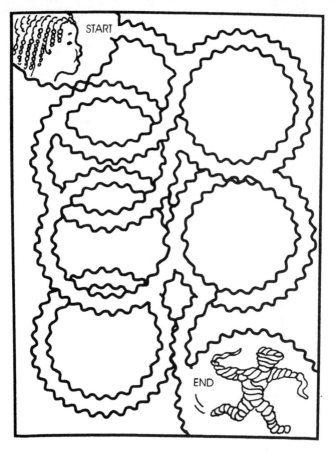

Wanda wonders if she really saw
a mummy. Help her find the answer.

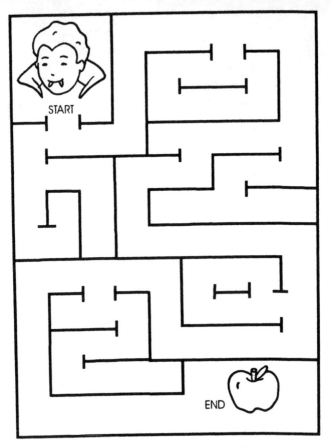

START

END

Can you help this Halloween Dracula
reach the delicious apple?

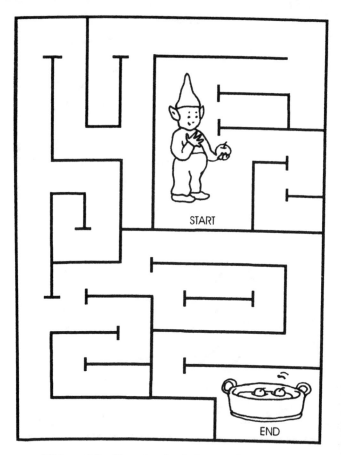

START

END

This goblin likes to dunk for apples. Show
him how to find the apple dunking corner.

Help one ghost find its friend
by following the path.

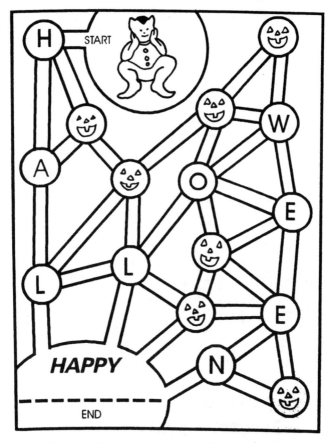

To complete the message, this goblin must collect the letters in the puzzle without crossing any pumpkins. Then write them in order in the blanks below.

41

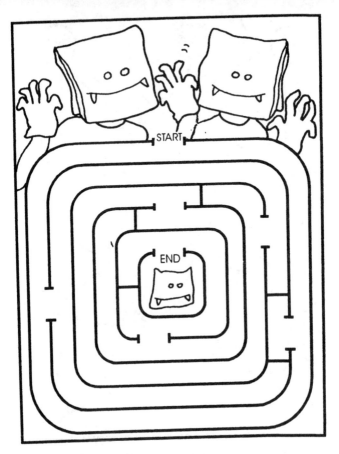

START

END

Show these two Halloweeners
how to find their friend.

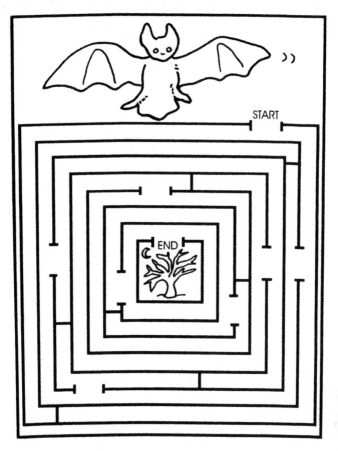

Help this bat find the path to its
favorite Halloween spot.

Chuck will take off his devil's mask so he
can eat some devil's food cake.
Help him find the cake.

START

END

This goblin says that pumpkins can be
found in the cornfield. Follow the path
to find out if he's right.

45

There is a hidden path that leads to
a haunted house. Can you find it?

Who is saying, "whoooo" on Halloween?
Follow the path to find out.

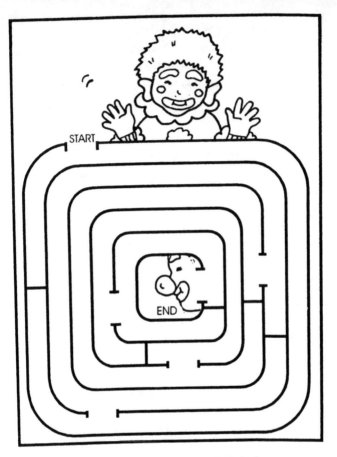

START

END

Something is missing on Billy's face.
Follow the path to find the answer.

Someone dressed as a gorilla needs more
balloons for a party. Help him find them.

Help the witch find the path that
leads to her Halloween friend.

A tiny seed was planted last summer
before Halloween. Find out what
happened when it grew.

Solutions

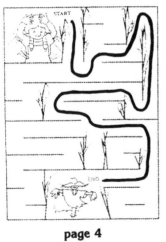

page 4

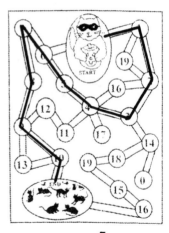

page 5

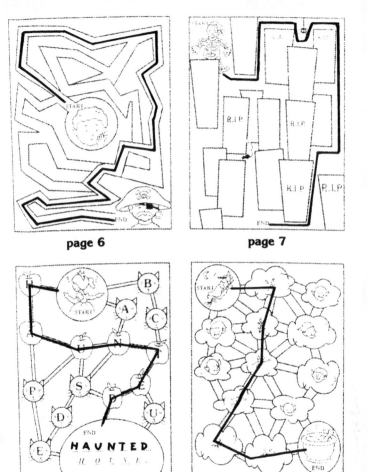

page 6

page 7

page 8

page 9

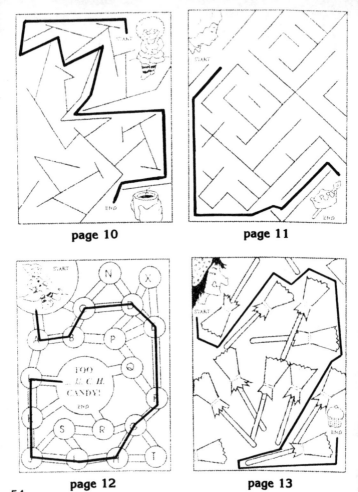

page 10

page 11

page 12

page 13

54

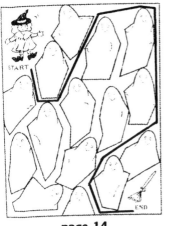

page 14

page 15

page 16

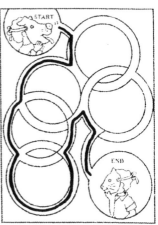

page 17

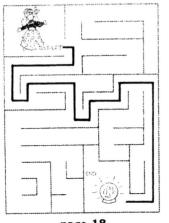

page 18

START

END

page 19

START

END

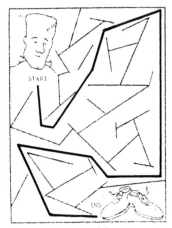

page 20

START

END

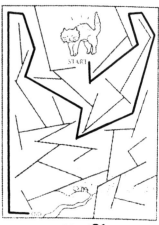

page 21

START

END

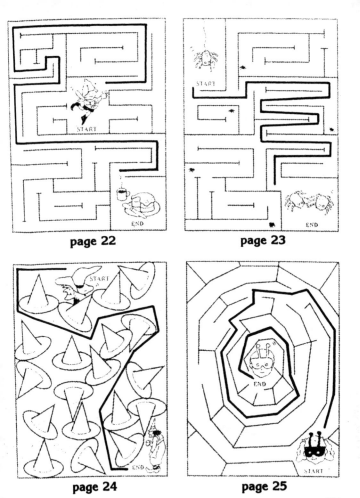

page 22

page 23

page 24

page 25

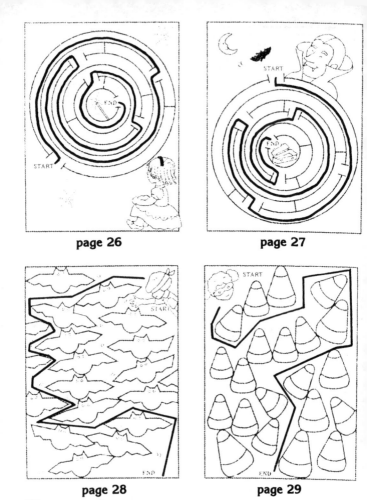

page 26

page 27

page 28

page 29

58

page 30

page 31

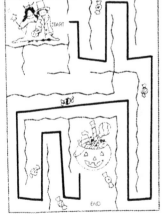

page 32

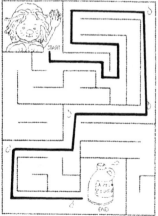

page 33

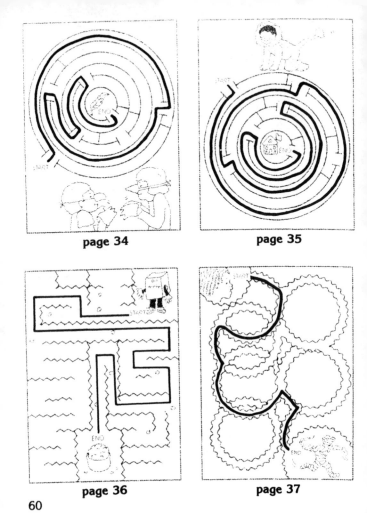

page 34

page 35

page 36

page 37

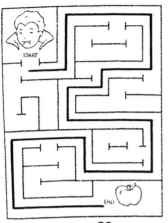

page 38

page 39

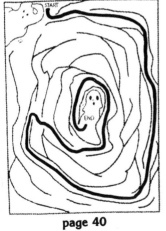

page 40

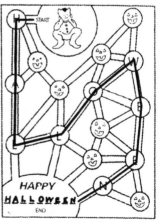

page 41

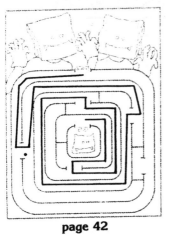

page 42

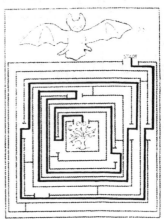

page 43

page 44

page 45

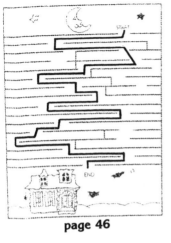

page 46

page 47

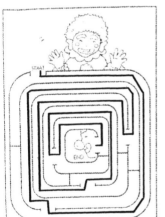

page 48

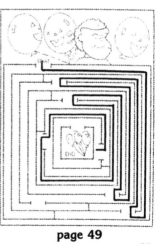

page 49

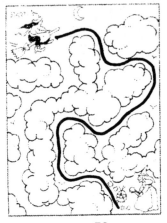

page 50

page 51